MALORIE BLACKMAN

The *Amazing Adventures* of

Girl
Wonder

Illustrated by Lis Toft

D1585946

BARN OWL BOOKS

These stories are selected from *Girl Wonder and the Terrific Twins* (Gollancz 1991) and *Girl Wonder to the Rescue* (Gollancz 1994) This edition was first published 2003 by Barn Owl Books 157 Fortis Green Road, London N10 3LX Barn Owl Books are distributed by Frances Lincoln 4 Torriano Mews, Torriano Avenue, London NW5 2RZ

ISBN 978-1-903015-27-8

Designed and typeset by Douglas Martin, Oadby Printed in China for Imago

The Amazing Adventures of Girl Wonder

Contents

To Neil, with love and affection, M.B.

The Mission to Rescue the Football

"Mum, can we play Catch in the garden?" I asked.

"Please, please," said my brother Antony.

"Please, *please*," said my other brother Edward.

Mum's head appeared from beneath the bonnet of her car. She wiped her oily hands on her overalls.

"All right then," Mum said. "But mind the fence by the tree, it's a bit loose. And for goodness sake, keep the ball away from Miss Ree's flowers."

Miss Ree is our moany, old next-door neighbour. She has flowers growing all around her smooth-as-paper lawn. She moans if we even breathe near her flowers. We call her Misery. Miss Ree . . . Mis-ery — get it?

The twins and I ran through the house,

grabbed the ball and ran out into the back garden.

It was hot, hot, hot with not a single cloud in the blue sky. We played Piggy-In-The-Middle and Catch for a while.

"I'm hot," complained Antony.

"I'm bored," complained Edward.

"Let's play football instead," I suggested. "We'll each be a team and you only score a goal if you hit the trunk of the apple tree."

"Yeah! football!" said Antony, clapping his hands.

"Yippee! Football," said Edward, jumping up and down.

We all like football.

I scored the first two goals, then Edward tripped me up and Antony got the ball.

"Cheats! Cheats!" I shouted, chasing after them.

Antony kicked the ball as hard as he could.

"Yah! You missed," I shouted.

Antony didn't miss the tree trunk by inches. He missed it by miles. The ball sailed over the fence into Miss Ree's Garden and landed with a SPLOP! Right in her flowerbed.

Antony, Edward and I ran to the fence and looked over.

Oh dear!

If we asked for our ball back, Miss Ree would complain to Mum and then we'd get told off.

So I said, "This is a job for Girl Wonder and . . ."

"The Terrific Twins – hooray!" the twins shouted.

We all spun around until we were getting giddy.

"OK, Terrific Twins, I've got a plan," I said. "We'll climb over the fence and I'll get the ball whilst you two watch for Misery. Make sure you warn me if she's coming."

"OK, Girl Wonder," said Antony.

So we all started to clamber over the fence.

CRR . . . RR . . . EAK!

CRR . . . RR . . . UNCH!

The whole fence fell flat – right on to Miss

Ree's flowerbed. And with us on top of it! We were sprawled out and wondering what had happened. Miss Ree's kitchen door burst open. Then our kitchen door was flung open.

"My roses! My lupins! My begonias!" Miss Ree wailed.

"My goodness!" Mum said, running out of the kitchen.

"Just look what they've done to my flowers." Miss Ree said to Mum. Mum put her hands on her hips. Her face was like dark grey clouds just before thunder and lightning.

"Maxine, Antony, Edward, what have you been doing now?" Mum said.

"We just wanted to get our ball, Mum," I said as we all stood up.

"I'm sorry about your flowers, Miss Ree," Mum said. "Don't worry. I'll fix the fence and we'll replace all the flowers."

Then Mum called us into the house.

She told us off in the kitchen. She told us off in the car as we drove to the garden centre. She told us off as we picked out new flowers and rose bushes. She told us off as we drove back home. She told us off as she fixed the fence. She told us off as we all pulled the scrushed, crushed flowers out of the ground and planted the new ones.

Whilst Mum was resting her mouth for a second, I whispered to Antony, "There's our ball. Run and get it and throw it back into our garden."

Before Mum could say anything, Antony did just that.

Once we had replanted Miss Ree's new flowers and rose bushes, Mum called us into the house again.

Can we take our ball and go to the park?" I asked.

"No you cannot. You three can stay in for the rest of the day and stay out of trouble," Mum said.

So after we'd washed our hands and faces and changed our clothes, the twins and I sat on the carpet in the living-room playing Snap.

"Your plan was stupid," Antony grumbled.

"Yeah! Silly-stupid," said Edward.

"But it worked, didn't it?" I said. "We did get our ball back!"

The Tooth Fairy Mystery

"Ow! Ouch!" My tooth was killing me! My whole right cheek was puffed up like a balloon.

"That does it, Maxine," said Mum. "If your tooth isn't out by tomorrow, I'm taking you to the dentist."

"Ouch! Ow!" My tooth hurt too much to even protest.

"Let me see it, Maxine," said Edward.

I opened my mouth and wobbled my loose tooth very, *very* gently to show him.

"Where? I can't see anything," Edward said.

"I . . . ri . . . th . . ." I said, with my mouth still wide open.

Edward frowned. "I still don't see anything."

I took my finger out of my mouth. "It's right there. It's the tooth I'm wobbling about," I frowned. "Can't you see it?"

Edward moved closer until his nose was practically in my mouth.

"I still don't see it," he complained.

I frowned at him. "What's the matter with your eyes?" I asked.

"Let me see," said Antony, barging Edward out of the way.

I showed Antony. He spotted my wobbly tooth immediately.

"When it comes out, put it under your pillow and then you'll get money from the tooth fairy," said Antony.

"Tooth fairy!" I scoffed. "There's no such thing as a tooth fairy. It's just Mum who puts money under your pillow when you lose a tooth."

"Is it?" Mum smiled. "You think so?"

"I know so," I said. "I caught you the last time, Mum – remember?"

"Ah, but that's why I got in touch with the Tooth Fairy Society and asked them to take over the job," said Mum.

"The Tooth Fairy Society?" said Edward.

"Mum's pulling your leg," I laughed.

"No I'm not, Maxine," Mum shook her head. "I won't be putting money under your pillow any more. Your own personal tooth fairy will be doing it from now on."

"I don't believe a word of it," I said.

Mum shrugged. "Suit yourself. But when your tooth falls out and you put it under your pillow, I won't be the one swapping it for money.

"Do we have our own personal tooth fairies too?" asked Antony, his eyes wide.

"Of course," smiled Mum.

"It's not true. It's just Mum who does it," I protested.

But from the look on Antony's and Edward's faces, it was clear that they believed Mum rather than me.

In a huff, I marched downstairs.

All afternoon as I sat watching telly, I wibbled and wobbled my tooth about. I turned it to the left and I turned it to the right and I wobbled it back and forth, back and forth. Until at last with a TWORP! it came out of my gum.

By now Mum, Edward and Antony had come downstairs. Mum gave me some warm salty

water in a glass. "Go upstairs to the bathroom and rinse your mouth out with that," said Mum. "It will kill infections but don't swallow any or it'll make you sick."

I went upstairs to gargle with the salty water. Now my tooth was out, my mouth didn't hurt at all.

That's more like it, I thought to myself.

Then I had an idea. If Antony and Edward didn't believe that Mum was the only tooth fairy in our house, then I would prove it to them.

"This is a job for Girl Wonder by herself!" I said to my reflection in the mirror. And I sloshed the last of the salty water around and around my mouth before spitting it out. I ran to my bedroom and put the tooth under my pillow before going back downstairs again.

"How are you feeling?" Mum asked.

"Fine!" I grinned. "What time will you be swapping my tooth for money, Mum?"

"I've already told you, Maxine, I don't do that any more," smiled Mum.

"Well, I'm going to wait up all night," I told her. "And if my tooth is still under my pillow by tomorrow morning then that will prove that tooth fairies don't exist."

"You'll never stay up all night," Mum laughed. "You, Maxine, are a girl who likes her sleep!"

And with that, off Mum went to get a glass of orange juice. Now was my chance.

"Terrific Twins, I need your help," I said to my brothers

"You do?" said Antony, surprised.

"Why?" said Edward.

"For what?" asked Antony.

"I want you two to help me look out for this so-called tooth fairy tonight." I whispered to them. "I'm going to prove that Mum and the tooth fairy are one and the same person."

"But why do you need us?" Edward asked.

"Because Mum's right! If I try to keep watch by myself, I'm only going to fall asleep," I replied. "But with your help, at least one of us will always be awake. There's no way Mum can sneak past all three of us."

"I'm not sure about this, Maxine," said Antony. "I like my sleep too!"

"So do I!" Edward agreed.

"Oh, come on. Do you want to catch Mum in the act or don't you?" I asked, crossly.

"OK then," my brothers agreed reluctantly, and we all spun around, bumping and bouncing and bashing into each other.

"Right then. Edward, you can hide behind the wardrobe and Antony, you can hide behind the curtains," I explained.

"And where will you be?" asked Antony.

"Yeah! Exactly where will you be?" Edward said.

"I'll be in bed of course," I said. "Where else would I be? We don't want Mum to get suspicious, do we?"

Antony and Edward frowned at each other.

"How come we get the hardest bit?" asked Antony.

"Yeah! How come?"

"Because it's my plan," I replied.

Just then Mum came into the room.

"What are you three up to now?" she said, her eyes narrowing.

"You'll see, Mum," I smiled. "You'll see."

Later that night, Antony stood behind the curtains and Edward stood by the wardrobe, hidden from the door. I sat up in bed, waving my torch about in the darkness.

"How long have we got to stand here?" asked Antony.

"Yeah! How long?" asked Edward.

"Until we catch Mum or the tooth fairy or both," I yawned.

"But my legs are getting tired," said Antony.

"And my eyelids are getting sleepy," said Edward. "I can hardly keep them open."

"Well, you must," I insisted with another yawn. "I'm just going to lie down here and pretend to be asleep so that when Mum comes in, she'll not suspect anything."

I snuggled down under my duvet whilst Edward and Antony grumbled and moaned about how they always had to do all the hard work. I struggled to keep my eyes open, I really did, but my pillow was soft and my bed was warm and my whole body was tired. So I thought, I'll just close my eyes – just for a couple of seconds.

The next thing I knew – it was morning! And Edward and Antony were nowhere in sight. I lifted up my pillow – and there it was. A bright, shiny twenty-pence piece. Rats! Mum must have sneaked in after I'd fallen asleep and Edward and Antony had gone back to their own bedroom.

I had a shower and went downstairs. Mum was already down there cooking breakfast.

"Morning, Maxine," she grinned.

"Morning, Mum," I said glumly.

"What's the matter with you? Didn't the tooth fairy visit?"

"I know you're the tooth fairy, Mum, so don't pretend you're not." I said.

And then Mum said something that completely threw me.

"Maxine, I give you my word that I haven't been in your room since yesterday afternoon," Mum said seriously. "Cross my heart and hope to die."

"But you must have," I frowned. "How did that twenty-pence piece get under my pillow then?"

Mum just shrugged.

I had a long, hard think.

"Well? Have you solved the mystery yet?"

Mum laughed.

"I think there are only three ways that money could have got under my pillow . . ." I began.

"Oh yes?"

"I put my tooth under my pillow yesterday afternoon when it came out. So either you guessed that I'd already put my tooth under my pillow and swapped it for the money yesterday afternoon . . ."

"Or?" prompted Mum.

"Or else Antony and Edward were in on it and they swapped my tooth for the money when I fell asleep last night . . ."

"Or?" asked Mum.

"Or else there really are tooth fairies!" I said.

Mum creased up laughing. "And which theory do you believe?" she asked.

"I'm not sure," I replied. "But one thing I *am* sure about – the next time one of my teeth falls out, I'm going to stay awake all night. All day and all night if I have to, until I solve the tooth fairy mystery!"

"We'll see!" laughed Mum. "We'll see."

The Birthday Box

It was Mum's birthday two and a half months after Christmas. The twins and I put our money together to buy Mum a present. We had just enough money to buy her a scarf and a card.

"It doesn't look like much," Antony frowned.

"Yeah, not much at all," Edward agreed glumly.

"It's all we can afford," I sighed.

"It's not very big," said Antony.

"It's not very chunky," complained Edward.

"It should look like *something* when it's wrapped up," Antony continued. "A scarf is going to look itchy-titchy."

They made it sound like it was my fault.

"So what should I do?" I asked crossly.

"I don't know," Antony replied. "You're Girl Wonder . . ."

"Well, you two are the Terrific Twins," I replied. "You think of something."

So we all spun around and around, not feeling very super at all. We sat on the floor cross-legged, staring at the scarf and trying to think of a way to make the scarf seem bigger and better than it was.

Then I had an extra-giga-brilliant idea.

"Let's wrap it in tons and tons of paper," I said. "Then it'll look big and chunky and more like *something*."

"Good idea," Antony agreed.

"Not bad," said Edward.

We ran downstairs. Mum was in the kitchen, taking the vacuum cleaner motor to pieces.

"Mum, we need a box," I said.

"A ginormous box," added Antony.

"A Humungous Box!" Edward said eagerly.

"Why?" asked Mum.

"We want to put your birthday present in it," Antony told her.

"Oh, I see . . ." Mum said slowly. "If you tell me what you've got me, then I'll be better able to judge what size of box would suit you best."

"We got you . . ."

"EDWARD! Don't tell her!" I interrupted quickly. "Mum, you'll have to wait until tomorrow to see what it is."

Mum mumbled something under her breath. It sounded like 'worth a try'. She looked in the cupboard under the sink.

"There's this box that held my writing paper," Mum suggested, taking a smallish box out from the cupboard.

"That's much too small," Antony said immediately.

"Yeah, far too small," Edward agreed.

Then Mum fished out a middling-sized box. "This box held all the bottles of lemonade and cream soda that we bought from the supermarket before Christmas."

"Still too small," I shook my head.

"Much too small," Antony said.

"Far too small," Edward agreed.

Mum looked surprised. She straightened up.

"The only other box I've got that's larger is the one the vacuum cleaner came in."

"That'll do," I replied.

"Just," Antony added.

"Only just," said Edward.

"What did you three buy me? A rhinoceros?" Mum frowned.

"You'll have to wait until tomorrow morning to find out," I said.

"Where's the vacuum cleaner box?" Antony asked.

"In the cupboard under the stairs," Mum replied. "Er . . . would you three like some help wrapping up my present?"

"No, thanks. We can manage," I said

We got the box out of the cupboard.

"Now we'll need some special paper to wrap the box with and we'll need some more paper to pad the box," I said.

"Oh? Is my present something that might break if you don't pad the box? Mum asked.

I hadn't realized she was listening behind us.

"Go away, Mum," I said crossly, my hands on my hips.

"I was only trying to help," Mum muttered, going back into the kitchen.

More like, she was only trying to be nosy!

Mum came out of the kitchen and handed us a whole roll of brown paper. "You can use this to stuff the box and to wrap it," she said.

Antony, Edward and I took the box and the brown paper and went upstairs. Half an hour later, we all sat back to admire our work. The box looked terrific! It was a bit of a shame it had only a scarf in it. We'd filled the box with crumpled, rumpled brown paper and put Mum's scarf right in the middle. The outside was brilliantly wrapped in more brown paper. We drew stars and moons and comets and space ships all over the brown paper and coloured them in. Then we carried the box downstairs.

"There you are, Mum," I said, as we plonked-down the box. "This is your birthday present."

31

"My goodness! What is it!" Mum said. She bent down and shook the box. It didn't make a sound.

"You'll have to wait until tomorrow to find out," Antony said.

"Yeah, tomorrow morning," said Edward.

"Can't I open it now?" Mum asked, giving it another shake.

"No, you can't. Wait until your birthday tomorrow," I said firmly.

"Oh, all right then," Mum said reluctantly. But she had a strange gleam in her eyes.

That night I was dreaming about flying through the air faster than a speeding rocket and leaping over giant trees with just one jump, when I heard a funny-peculiar noise. It woke me up. I listened. The house was very quiet. I wondered if maybe I'd dreamt the noise. Deciding I must have dreamt it, I pulled my duvet up around my ears and snuggled down to go back to sleep.

Then I heard the same noise again. The stairs were creaking. We were being burgled!

The Birthday Burglar

I sat up, listening in the darkness. I heard another creak from one of the bottom steps. We were definitely being burgled. I got out of bed and tiptoed out of my room. I was scared – so scared – but I was a super-hero and we super-heroes have to be braver than brave. I went into the twins' room. They were fast asleep. I might have guessed. It would take fifteen planes flying over our house at the same time to wake those two up.

"Come on, you two. Wake up!" I whispered. "We're being burgled, so this is definitely a job for Girl Wonder . . ."

"And the Terrific Twins?" Antony whispered back, instantly awake. "Isn't this more a job for the police?"

"Definitely a job for Mum or the police," agreed Edward. "Or a grown-up."

"No, I've got a plan," I said.

My brothers got out of their bunk-beds and we whirled and twirled around quickly but quietly, so that the burglar wouldn't hear us.

33

Luckily there was a full moon so we had the moonlight to see by, otherwise the twins would have tripped over their own feet and made all kinds of noise. I whispered my plan to them. Then we crept slowly and silently down the stairs. We got to the living room. I could hear

noises. There was definitely someone in there, trying their best not to make a sound. We crept to the open living room door.

"Ready, Terrific Twins . . .?" I whispered.

"Ready, Girl Wonder . . ." the Terrific Twins whispered back.

"Go!"

The Terrific Twins pulled the living-room door shut, then I quickly turned the key in the lock, locking the door. I switched on the hall light, because with the living-room door shut, you can't see much in the hall.

"Right then, Mr Burglar!" I called out. "We have you now! And don't even think about getting out through the window, because Mum puts locks on all the windows in the house and the window key is in the kitchen."

The Terrific Twins were jumping up and down now.

"Hooray! We caught a burglar," Antony shouted.

"All by ourselves," Edward yelled, "Yippee!"

"Antony, you go and get Mum. Edward, you watch the door. I'll phone the police . . ."

"Maxine . . . MAXINE! Let me out of here THIS SECOND!"

We stared at the locked living-room door.

"Mum . . . Mum, is that you?" I asked, surprised.

"OF COURSE IT'S ME. OPEN THE DOOR! NOW!" Mum didn't sound too pleased at all.

We were in seriously, serious trouble. Possibly the most seriously, serious trouble we'd ever been in. I unlocked the door.

Sparks flew from Mum's eyes.

"What do you three think you're playing at?" Mum asked furiously, her hands on her hips.

"I heard a noise, Mum," I said. "We thought you were a burglar."

"A burglar . . ." Mum spluttered. "If . . . if you thought you'd heard a burglar in this house you should have come to wake me up first, not tackled him by yourselves. And what do you mean by locking me in the living room?"

"We couldn't let you escape, Mum," Antony said. "Not when we thought you were a burglar."

Antony edged past Mum to look in the living- room. I think he still couldn't believe there was no burglar.

"Right! No pocket money for a month for any of you," Mum said. "In fact, no pocket money ever again!"

"But Mum . . ." I said, dismayed.

"Wait a minute, Mum. What's the matter with your present?" Antony asked.

"What? Er . . . nothing." Mum tried to shoo

Antony out of the living-room. I sneaked past her to take a look. The wrapping paper of Mum's present was open at the top.

"I . . . I must have tripped over it in the dark and accidentally opened it," Mum said quickly.

We looked at her. Mum had been doing a spot of burgling!

"Come on Terrific Twins, let's go back to bed," I said.

"But Mum's been opening . . ." Antony began.

"But Mum's present is . . ." started Edward.

"I think you two must have been dreaming," I said to the Terrific Twins. "Mum wouldn't be so sneaky as to try and open her birthday present before her birthday. Isn't that right, Mum?"

"Absolutely right, Maxine," Mum agreed.

"I mean, Mum warned us against opening our Christmas presents before Christmas Day – remember? So she wouldn't do the same thing herself," I continued.

"Never mind Mum's present! What about our pocket money?" Antony wailed.

"Yeah, our pocket money?" said Edward, dismayed. "This is all your fault, Maxine. It was your flimsy-floppy-drippy-droopy idea to catch the burglar."

I looked up at Mum.

"Mum, you said . . ." I got no further.

"I never said anything about your pocket money. You three are dreaming! Now go back to bed!"

"Are you coming too?" I asked Mum.

"Yes, I am. I've had enough excitement for one night. I think we all have," said Mum, shaking her head and yawning.

I stuck down the wrapping paper again on Mum's present and we all went to bed.

The next morning when Mum finally opened her present and found her scarf, she liked it.

"We put it in a big box because it was only a little present," I explained.

"Size has nothing to do with it. Big things aren't the best things just because they're big," Mum said. "I love this scarf. It's so pretty and just the thing for the spring chill."

We all went for a walk to the park so that Mum could try it out. Hooray for spring! We all love the spring!

It means summer's just round the corner.

Rescuing the Rescuers

"I want a dog," I said.

"I want a cat," said Antony.

"I want a rabbit," said Edward.

Mum put her hands on her hips. I'm not getting three different pets. In fact I'm not sure I should get even one."

"But . . ." I said.

"But . . ." said Antony.

"But . . ." Edward repeated.

"No buts!" Mum argued. "I don't think you three realize how much work is involved in owning a pet."

"We do!" I said.

"We do!" said Antony.

"We do!" Edward repeated.

Then mum got a funny look in her eyes. The same look she gets when she has one of her ideas and she thinks it's a good one.

I wonder why her ideas always seem to get me and the twins into trouble?

"Stay there you three. I'll be right back," Mum said, and off she dashed.

My brothers and I looked at each other and shrugged. Before we got bored just standing and waiting, Mum came back with a large box in her hands.

"What's in the box?" we asked.

Mum put the box down on the carpet. We peered into it.

"A cat!" I said, surprised.

"It's Mr McBain's cat. Her name is Syrup because she's the exact same colour as golden syrup."

Mr McBain is our other next-door neighbour. He's a tall, elderly man with hair that only grows on the sides of his head. The top of his head is shiny and smooth like an egg.

"How come we've got her?" Antony asked.

"Yeah! How come?" asked Edward.

"If you three can look after Syrup for this weekend without getting into trouble then we'll talk seriously about which pet to get – but only then," Mum said.

"What do we do first?" I asked.

Antony, Edward and I knelt down round the box.

"First, take Syrup out of the box. Then take her litter tray out of the box and put it in the conservatory near the washing machine. Then you can feed her. Mr McBain also gave me two tins of cat food. They're in my trouser pockets. After that you can play with her," Mum said.

So I picked Syrup out of the box and held her against my chest and stroked her. She was warm and her fur was soft. Her breath tickled my face. I liked her.

"Maybe we should have a cat and not a dog," I thought.

Antony took out Syrup's litter tray and put it in the conservatory. Edward got the two tins of cat food out of Mum's tracksuit trouser pockets.

"Later on we'll all have to pop to the shop at the top of the road and get some more cat food," said Mum.

Mum opened one of the tins and put the food in Syrup's bowl which was also in the box. We all crouched down around Syrup as she ate.

"I want a cat, Mum," I said.

"So do I," Antony said.

"Yeah! Me too!" said Edward.

"We'll see," was all Mum said.

After Syrup had eaten her lunch we took her outside whilst Mum went to watch the telly. I was still holding her.

"Syrup, this is our garden." I said.

"Miaow!" Syrup replied, having a look around.

Then, before any of us had a chance to blink, Syrup struggled out of my arms, scurried across our garden and scooted up our apple tree.

"What do we do now?" Antony asked.

"Yeah! What?" asked Edward.

"We can't call Mum," I said. "She'll say we can't look after a pet for one minute without getting into trouble."

"So what *are* we going to do?" asked Antony.

"Yeah! What?" Edward repeated.

So I said, "This is a job for Girl Wonder and . . ."

"The Terrific Twins!" Antony and Edward grinned.

Then we all spun around until we were dizzy.

"All right, Terrific Twins, I have a plan," I said. "We'll climb up the tree and get Syrup down."

And that's what we did. Slowly and carefully, we each climbed up the tree. (I helped the twins get on to the first branch as they couldn't quite reach it.) Up and up we went.

Up and up. And above us I could see Syrup staring down at us.

Just as we got close to her, guess what she did?

She yawned. She stretched her back. Then she scooted *down* the tree.

"Huh! Why didn't she do that *before* we came up here?" I said.

We all looked down. The ground looked far, *far* away.

"What are you kids up to?" Mr McBain called out from his garden.

"What do you children think you're doing?" shouted Miss Ree from her garden. "Get down at once before you hurt yourselves."

I looked at Antony and Edward and they looked at me. Then we all burst into tears.

"We can't get down," I sobbed. "The ground is far, far away."

Then Mum came running out into the garden.

"Maxine, Antony, Edward, what have you been doing now?" she said, her hands on her hips.

"We were trying to rescue the cat," I sniffed.

"Maxine, cats climb up trees all the time. Unlike you lot, they have no trouble climbing down either. You should have left Syrup up there." Mr McBain said.

"Mum, I want to come down," wailed Antony.

"Yeah! Me too!" Edward joined in.

"I'm going to have to call the Fire Brigade," Mum said.

Within minutes we heard the sound of the fire engine siren – DRING DRING DRING DRING! Mum ran into the house to let them in. Seconds later she came out into the garden followed by a firewoman and three firemen.

They all stood below our apple tree. We peered down at them. We'd never seen firepeople up close before. The firemen placed two ladders against the trunk of the tree.

"It's all right. We'll soon have you down," said the firewoman.

"Don't worry," said one of the firemen. "You'll soon be on the ground."

They carried Antony and Edward down first. I looked around. I could see across all the neighbours' gardens. *Everyone* was watching us.

"All right, Maxine, take my hands," said the firewoman, lifting me round on to her back. "I'm going to give you a piggyback ride. In Scotland we call it a collybucky."

"A collybucky! That's a funny name." I laughed.

"No funnier than piggyback," said the fire-woman. "Here we are down on the ground."

I looked around, surprised. I hadn't even noticed us coming down.

"Say thank you to the firepeople," Mum said.

"Thank you very much," we said.

"Right, you three – go into the house. I've got a few things to say to you," Mum said sternly. "And Syrup is going straight back to Mr McBain."

We went into the kitchen and looked through the window. Mum was talking to the firepeople.

"Mum's going to spend for ever telling us off now," Antony said to me, annoyed.

"Yeah! For ever!" Edward agreed.

"Your plan was stinky," Antony grumbled.

"Yeah! Seriously stinky," Edward mumbled.

"But it worked, didn't it?" I said. "We *did* get Syrup out of the tree."

As Tall as Tall

I was in a bad mood when I got home from school.

"What's the matter with you?" Antony asked?

"Yeah, what's the matter?" asked Edward.

I stared at myself in the hall mirror. I turned to the left and I turned to the right.

"Do you think I'm short?" I asked my brothers.

"You're taller than us," said Antony.

"A lot taller," agreed Edward.

"But I'm not as tall as Sharon in my class at school. She's taller than everyone – except the teacher."

"So?" said Antony.

"She called me a short dumpling," I frowned. "I need to grow taller – a lot taller. I want to be taller than Sharon. I want to be as tall as tall."

"How are you going to do that?" Antony asked.

"Yeah, how?" asked Edward.

"I'll have to think about that one," I replied.

"Maybe this is a job for Girl Wonder and . . ."

"The Terrific Twins!" my brothers shouted, whirling around like spinning tops.

"We need a plan – something that will make me grow," I said. "Come on Terrific Twins – I need your help. Think!"

We sat down on the carpet, each of us crossing our legs. We each sat very still and thought and thought. I thought so hard that my eyes began to ache.

"How tall do you want to grow?" asked Antony. "Do you want to grow as tall as a mountain or only as tall as a tree?"

I thought for a moment. "As tall as a tree," I decided.

That would be tall enough.

We each thought some more.

"Well, if you plant a little seed it grows into a big tree," Edward said. "So maybe if you swallowed a little seed, it would grow into a big tree inside you and it would push you up and up and then you'd be as tall as a tree. You'd be as tall as tall."

"That's a good idea!" I grinned. "I'll swallow orange seeds. Orange trees are tall and I can get the seeds because we always have plenty of oranges in the house. Are you two going to join me?"

"Nah! We'll watch you first to see if it works," Antony said.

"Yeah, we'll watch you first," Edward agreed.

Just then Mum came in from the garage.

"Right then. What would you three like for your tea?" Mum asked.

"Fish and chips," said Antony.

"Sausages and chips," said Edward, clapping his hands.

"Oranges," I shouted.

Mum just laughed. I think she thought I was joking.

In the end Mum made fish and chips. I didn't have any even though it smelt scrummy-delicious. I had to leave room for my oranges. Whilst the twins and Mum scoffed the scrummy-delicious fish and chips I chewed on my oranges, swallowing the seeds whole.

"Why are you eating so many oranges?" Mum asked me.

"I like oranges," I replied, trying to force down the last orange.

Mum looked at me, her eyes suspicious.

All she said was "Hhmm."

The next day I had two oranges for breakfast, three oranges for lunch and four oranges for dinner. As soon as dinner was finished I

measured myself against our measuring wall in the bathroom. I hadn't grown one millimetre! And what's more I was sick – sick of oranges.

When I woke up the next morning I had the worst tummy ache in the world.

"Ooh!" I groaned. "Ooooh!"

Mum called the doctor.

"Now then, Maxine," Doctor Turner said after taking my temperature, "your mum told me that you're eating a lot of oranges. She said you're eating oranges and nothing else. Is that right?"

I nodded. Oooooooh! My stomach was really hurting.

"Why have you suddenly become so keen on oranges?" Doctor Turner asked.

Mum was glaring at me from beside Doctor Turner. She had her hands on her hips.

"I love oranges." I didn't exactly lie, but I didn't exactly tell the truth either.

"Is that the *whole* reason?" Mum asked softly.

I thought hard. My stomach ache was getting worse and I was as miserable as miserable but I didn't want to tell Mum why I was eating so many oranges. She might stop me, or worse still she might get annoyed.

"Yeah, that's the whole reason," I replied.

"Doctor Turner, can I speak to you for a moment?" Mum said.

The doctor and my mum went outside my room to stand on the landing.

"I . . . oranges . . . cure . . . oranges . . . oranges . . . oranges . . ." That was all I heard, even though I pushed my ears as far forward as possible.

Mum and Doctor Turner came back into the room.

"Maxine, Doctor Turner agrees with me that what you need is a diet of oranges and nothing else," Mum began. "I *was* going to make you a cheese, onion and potato pie, followed by ice-cream and chocolate sauce and a long glass of ice-cold cream soda, but . . ."

"It's all right," I said quickly, "I don't mind having that."

"Nonsense," Mum smiled. "You said you love

oranges. That's all you've eaten for the last two days."

"But just to make sure that Maxine gets all her essential vitamins and minerals, I would prescribe two tablespoons of cod-liver oil three times a day and a chewy vitamin tablet twice a day," said Doctor Turner, scribbling on a pad. "That way Maxine can eat as many oranges as she likes and nothing else."

"NO! I DON'T WANT ANY MORE ORANGES," I pleaded. "Maybe . . . maybe I'm not so keen on them after all."

"Then why were you eating so many of them?" Mum asked.

Her eyes were glinting and sparkling like when the sun shines on water. When she looks at me like that, it's as if she can read my mind. I decided that perhaps I should just tell the truth. The truth takes a lot less effort.

"Well . . . Sharon at school called me a short dumpling," I muttered. "So I was swallowing orange seeds so that they would grow into a tree inside me and push me up. Then I'd be taller than Sharon and she couldn't call me a short dumpling any more."

"Oh, I see." Doctor Turner laughed.

"Oh, I see." Mum smiled.

"Maxine, it's the oranges that are causing your stomach ache," Doctor Turner said. "And it doesn't matter how many you eat, you'll never get a tree growing inside of you. If you want to grow you have to eat lots of different kinds of food – like carrots and greens, and protein foods like eggs and milk."

"Yuk!" I said. "What about chocolate? Will that make me grow?"

"Only sideways, not upwards," smiled Doctor Turner.

"Maxine, you're not short and it wouldn't matter if you were," Mum said. "It's what you are inside that counts, not what you are outside. Do you understand?"

"Yes, Mum," I said, holding my aching stomach.

"OK, Maxine, I'll prescribe some medicine for you which should take away your stomach ache. No more oranges or you'll turn into one," said Doctor Turner, pulling a face.

I smiled up at her. She's funny.

Mum went downstairs, followed by the doctor. After a few minutes Mum came back up the stairs alone, her hands behind her back.

"I've brought you a drink." Mum smiled, her eyes glinting.

"What is it?" I asked suspiciously.

Mum brought out the glass from behind her back. "Orange juice!" She laughed.

I buried my head under my pillow. "Take it away!" I said. "I never want to see anything that's orange ever again."

Antony and the Rap Attack

"What's the time, Mum?" I asked, wondering what had happened to our dinner. Mum had given us an apple each to keep us going until our dinner had finished cooking.

"Maxine wants more!
She's big as a door
And wide as the floor
So it's half-past four!" rapped Antony.

I gave my brother a dirty look.

"Maxine, it's ten minutes past six," sighed Mum. "Antony, how much longer are you going to say everything in rhyme?"

"If I'm a poet,
I've got to show it!
But I won't blow it!
You know it! You know it!" said Antony.

"Mum, tell him!" said Edward, covering his ears with his hands and pulling a face.

Antony was driving us all up the wall and on to the roof! For the last three days, all he'd done was talk in rhymes and raps, raps and rhymes. At first it was fun. Now it was getting on every

single one of my nerves.

"You're all just jealous," grinned Antony.

"Pinch me, someone! I must be dreaming. I thought I heard Antony say something that didn't rhyme!" Mum collapsed back on the sofa.

"I just suggest
That I'm the best.
I beat the rest,
So put me to the test!" rapped Antony.

"How about if I beat you over the head with this cushion?" I scowled at him.

"Mum, tell him!" said Edward.

Mum closed her eyes and put her hand to her temples. She stood up.

"I'm going to my bedroom to read," Mum said very quietly. "And you three are going to stay down here."

"Don't leave us with him," I begged Mum.

"Yeah, you can't leave us alone with him," Edward pleaded.

Antony started blowing raspberries and patting his cheeks.

"My name's not Freddy,
The dinner isn't ready!
It's got to cook.
Mum's off the hook.
She's going to her bed to read her library book!" Antony told us.

"I'll see you three when the dinner's ready," said Mum, even more quietly than before.

And before I could even blink, she was out of the room. I looked at Edward. Edward looked at me.

"Maxine, do something. Save me!" Edward put a cushion over his head, bending the corners down to cover his ears.

I turned to Antony. "If you make up one more rhyme, I'll . . . I'll . . ."

"I'm off to the loo!
But don't worry 'bout that.
'Cause before you know it,
I'll be back!" said Antony.

And off he went.

"Maxine, do something – *please*," Edward begged me.

"Come on, Edward," I said. "This is a job for G
Wonder . . ."

"And one of the Terrific Twins who's getting a
headache," Edward complained.

We whizzed-whirled around until we fell over.

"What's you plan?" asked Edward.

"I haven't actually got one yet," I admitted.

"Then think of one – fast," Edward ordered.

I thought and thought and thought. And at last
plan leapt into my head. I told Edward, just as
Antony came running down the stairs. Antony bu
into the room, but before he could say a word, I
in before him.

"Until you stop rhyming . . ." I began.

"Yeah, until you do . . ." said Edward.

Then Edward and I said together:

"We've decided

Not to talk to you."

Antony frowned at us.

"But there's nothing finer,

Than to be a rhymer . . ." he began.

Edward and I didn't let him finish. We said again,

"Until you stop rhyming,

Yeah, until you do,

We've decided

Not to talk to you."

"Come on, Edward. D'you fancy playing a video game?" I asked, ignoring Antony completely.

"Yes, all right," said Edward.

Edward switched on the telly and put our favourite video game into the game console.

"Me first," I said, picking up the controls.

"If you're no good at this

It won't be much fun.

So let me show you,

How it should be done!" said Antony.

I looked around the room, puzzled. "Funny! I thought I heard something," I said.

"So did I," said Edward. Then he shrugged. "We must be imagining things."

It was really mean, I know, but Antony was

driving us bonkers!

Antony looked at us.

"Can I play?" he said at last.

I looked at him. "No more rapping or rhyming?" I asked.

"No more rapping or rhyming," Antony said glumly.

"Thank goodness." Edward breathed a sigh of relief.

"You two just don't appreciate talent," said Antony.

"If you had any, we'd appreciate it," I answered.

Hhmm! Well, you'll both be sorry," Antony told us. "You're going to miss all my rhymes."

Edward and I fell about laughing.

"You must be joking!" we told him.

And we each took it in turns to play our video game. Our plan had worked. We'd finally got Antony to shut up!

For the rest of the day Antony was very quiet. I think he missed making up his rhymes. I didn't.

But the very next day, Edward and I were forced to eat our words.

The Zappers!

The next morning, the moment we walked into school, we knew that something was going on. Charlotte, my best friend, dashed over to me.

"Have you heard the news?" she asked.

"What news?" I said.

"There are notices like this all over the school.

WANTED

Singers, dancers, musicians, magicians – calling any and all performers for the school talent show – to be held in two weeks' time.
Auditions will be held this lunch-time in the assembly hall.

Mrs Kelsey – *Headmistress*

Are you going to try for it, Maxine?" Charlotte asked me, very excited.

"I don't know. A talent show . . . That'll be fun," I said.

"Maxine, we must go for it," said Edward, excited. "Wow! A talent show,"

"We've got to try," Antony agreed.

"But what are we going to do?" I said. "Has anyone got any ideas?"

Antony and Edward shook their heads.

We wandered away from the notice-board and out into the playground.

"I could sing," Edward suggested.

"Only if you want to get us booed off the stage," Antony wrinkled up his nose.

He was quite right too! Edward sings like a frog with a sore throat! Still his voice is better than mine, so maybe I shouldn't say much.

"How about dancing?" said Antony. "We could always do a dance."

"Ballet dancing," I asked, doubtfully.

Antony and Edward started jumping around, their arms waving about in the air like tree branches in a force twelve hurricane.

"How does this look?" asked Antony anxiously.

"Yeah, how does this look?" asked Edward.

"Like we need a few more lessons before we dance for anyone else," I sighed.

"Ballet dancing is hard work," Antony gasped.

"Maxine, what are we going to do?" asked Edward.

So I said, "That is a job for Girl Wonder . . ."

"And the Terrific Twins," said my brothers. And we all did ballet pirouettes and jumps until I landed on Antony's left foot by accident!

Then I had the best idea of my life.

"I've got it." I clapped my hands and waved them in the air over my head. "I've got it! I've got it!"

"What?" said Antony.

"Got what?" Edward repeated.

"Antony, you can do one of your rapping

rhymes and Edward and I will do the backing vocals and dances. If we practise at break-time, we'll be ready for the auditions at lunch-time," I grinned.

"A brilliant idea," said Edward.

"Extra-super-duper brilliant," I agreed.

But Antony didn't say a word.

"What's the matter, Antony?" I asked. "Don't you like my idea?"

"You two told me yesterday to stop making up rhymes and raps," Antony reminded us.

"That was yesterday," I said.

"Yeah, and this is today." Edward added.

"I'm not going to do it," said Antony. And he walked off!

I looked at Edward and he looked at me and we both ran after Antony.

"Antony, what're you talking about? "I frowned. "You have to do it. We haven't got time to practise anything else and you're brilliant at rhyming."

"That's not what you said yesterday," said Antony. "You said I didn't have any talent."

"No, we didn't . . ." I began, but Antony wouldn't let me finish.

"You said I didn't have any talent, because if I did you'd appreciate it," Antony said huffily.

"We do appreciate it, don't we, Maxine?" Edward said.

"Prove it," said Antony.

"Prove it? How?" I asked.

Then Antony got a glittering gleam in his eye.

Oh-oh! I thought. Oh-oh! I don't like the look of this.

"I'm not going to make up any more raps or rhymes until you two promise never to ask me to stop doing them . . ." Antony began.

"We promise," I said.

"Yeah, we definitely promise," Edward agreed.

"And until you both go down on your knees and say I've got lots and lots of talent!"

What could we do? I did'nt want to go down on my knees to Antony but I wanted to audition for the talent show. With Antony's help I was sure we'd be chosen, but without Antony . . .

"This is your fault, Maxine," Edward told me frostily. "It was your dippy-dorky-dozy idea to get Antony to stop making up rhymes yesterday."

"Edward, you wanted him to shut up just as much as I did," I said.

"I'm waiting," sniffed Antony, his nose in the air.

Edward and I looked at each other. Slowly we both got down on our knees.

"Dear Antony, you have got kilo-tons of talent," I said.

"Mega-tons," Edward agreed. "Maxine, what's bigger than mega-tons?"

"Giga-tons!" I replied. "So please say you'll do it."

"Very well, then," Antony said, at last, "Since you both asked so nicely."

I got to my feet, brushing off my kneecaps.

"I told you that you'd both be sorry and that you'd miss my rhymes," said Antony smugly.

"Antony," I said. "Don't rub it in."

But he did!

All through the morning break, we practised and practised. Antony came up with all the rhymes we should say, I invented the dance steps and Edward made up all the drum noises.

At last it was lunch time. We watched some of the other acts whilst we waited for our turn. One boy read out a poem about some clouds. At least five different people played tunes on their recorders. One boy played his violin. Three of the girls from my class had got together and they did an acrobatics show on the stage, which was quite good. Then it was our turn.

"So what do you call your act?" asked Mrs Kelsey, from in front of the stage.

I looked at the twins. They looked at me. We hadn't thought about that bit!

"Hang on a second," I said quickly. Antony, Edward and I bent in a huddle to discuss it. "We're called the Zappers!" I said at last.

"OK, Zappers," smiled Mrs Kelsey "Whenever

you're ready."

Antony stepped forward. I was on one side of him, Edward was on the other. Antony coughed to clear his throat. I counted out – just like I'd seen them do on the telly. "One, two, one, two, three, four."

And then we began.

Edward started slapping on his puffed-out cheeks. I started drumming on my chest and making rhythmic raspberry noises! We all started dancing, using the steps we'd rehearsed in the playground. Then Antony began.

"My name is Tony,
You know it's true,
We've got a lot
To say to you.
With my sister, Max,
And my brother, Ed,
If you don't like this
You must be dead!"

I started snapping my fingers whilst Edward took over the drum noises by slapping his chest.

"We're called the Zappers
We're finger-snappers
And great toe-tappers,
We're the youngest rappers!" rhymed Antony.

I smiled at him. He'd made up a whole new verse, just like that. What a hero.

Then it was Edward's turn. He stepped forward and started snapping his fingers.

"So don't try to stop us,

Or even top us.

'Cause we won't lose it,

We're busy making music!" rapped Edward.

"We won't cause a scene

We won't make a fuss

If you, Mrs Kelsey,

Will just choose us." We all said together. "Yeah!"

And with that we all did the splits – well, as close as we could get to them!

Mrs Kelsey and all the others in the hall started clapping and cheering and whistling. I grinned at Antony and Edward. They beamed back at me.

"You three are definitely going to be in the show!" Mrs Kelsey told us at once. And she hadn't said that to anyone else as soon as they'd finished. She'd told everyone else that they'd get her final decision by the end of the day.

"For once, one of your dizzy-dopey plans

actually worked, Maxine," said Edward, amazed.

"Thanks to Antony, the most supreme, the most excellent rapper in the universe!" I grinned.

And I meant it too!

Saving Energy

When I got home from school, I ran into the kitchen where Mum was mashing potatoes for our tea and the twins were laying the table.

"What did you do at school today?" Mum asked me.

"We learnt about energy and how we should all save it," I replied, dropping my school bag on the kitchen lino. "We should always switch off lights when we're not in the room and we should switch off all electric appli . . . appli . . . appliances when we're not using them."

"Quite right too," Mum said. "Mind you, I've been telling you and your brothers to save energy for years and you haven't listened to one word yet."

"Oh, we will now," I said.

"Why?" Antony asked.

"Yeah, why?" Edward repeated.

"Because the more energy we save the longer it will last us and the less we waste."

"What sort of waste?" Antony asked.

"Well . . ."

"Maxine means things like not filling a kettle with water when all you want is one cup of tea. It takes more energy and longer to heat up a full kettle than a half full one," Mum said.

"Hhmm!" Edward said.

"Maxine, could you spoon out the mashed potato on to the plates next to the sausages. I'll be right back."

When Mum left the rom, I said to the twins, "I think we should make sure that we save energy."

"How," Edward said, for once getting in before Antony.

"Hhmm!" I thought. "We're going to need a good plan. I think maybe this is a job for Girl Wonder . . ."

"And the Terrific Twins! Yippee!" shouted the twins. and we spun round until we all fell down.

"How about . . . how about if we make sure that everything is switched off before we go to bed tonight?" Antony suggested.

"We could go into each room and make sure that all the lights and things are switched off," Edward continued.

"That sounds like a good idea," I grinned. "All right then, I'll do upstairs and you two can do downstairs."

"How come we get the downstairs." Antony protested.

"Yeah, how come?" repeated Edward.

"Because downstairs is bigger and there are two of you," I explained.

"Hhmm!" they both said, but they didn't

argue so I got away with it.

After our tea of fat sausages and peas and mashed potatoes, we all sat down to watch telly.

"Mum, shouldn't we switch off the telly to save energy?" Edward asked.

Mum laughed. "But we're watching it. We can't save energy by switching it off and watch it at the same time."

"But it would save energy if we did switch it off, wouldn't it?" Edward persisted.

"Yes it would," Mum agreed. "But I'm not going to. I like this programme."

Edward leaned over and whispered to Antony and me. "Let's not watch it. Let's do something else – then that would save energy."

"I don't think it works like that," I frowned. "The telly uses the same amount of energy whether only Mum watches it or all four of us watch it."

So we watched telly until it was time for us to go to bed.

"I'm a bit tired, so I think I'll have an early night as well," Mum yawned, switching off the telly and pulling out the plug.

We cleaned our teeth and put on our pyjamas. Then, when Mum was in the bathroom, I grabbed my brothers.

"Come on Terrific Twins. Now's our chance to save energy. You two do the kitchen and the conservatory and the living-room and I'll do the bedrooms," I said.

Five minutes later we met back upstairs.

"We've saved energy everywhere," The twins said proudly.

"So have I," I said. "Goodnight Antony, goodnight Edward. See you in the morning."

"Mum read to the twins first, then she came into my bedroom and read me a fairy story. I love fairy stories.

"Goodnight Maxine." Mum smiled, and she switched off the bedroom light and closed the

door behind her. Then I fell asleep, dreaming of the ways I could save energy.

"MAXINE, ANTONY, EDWARD — GET DOWN HERE! THIS MINUTE!"

I rubbed my eyes. It was morning but I was still sleepy.

"MAXINE! EDWARD! ANTONY! NOW!"

I didn't like the sound of Mum's voice. It sounded crosser than cross. I hopped out of bed and walked down the stairs behind the twins.

"What's the matter?" I whispered to them.

"I don't know," Antony whispered back.

"Nor do I," Edward mouthed.

We walked into the kitchen where Mum was. Her hands were folded across her chest and her eyes were glaring at us.

I knew we were in BIG
TROUBLE.

"Which one of you ninnies
switched off the fridge last
night?" Mum asked.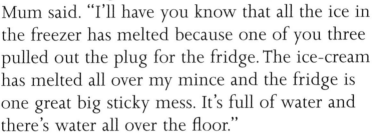

I looked at the twins. They
looked at me. No one spoke.

"I'm waiting for an answer,"
Mum said. "I'll have you know that all the ice in
the freezer has melted because one of you three
pulled out the plug for the fridge. The ice-cream
has melted all over my mince and the fridge is
one great big sticky mess. It's full of water and
there's water all over the floor."

Still no one said a word.

"And which one of you twits switched off the
washing machine when it was in the middle of
washing my jumpers?" Mum ranted. "Now all
my jumpers have shrunk. They're ruined."

The twins and I looked at each other. We
stayed silent.

"And which of you pea-heads pulled out the
plug for the video recorder. I wanted to tape a
late night film and I MISSED IT!"

Antony started to sniff, then to sob. "I . . . I
pulled out the plug for the fridge. I was only

trying to save energy like Maxine said. And I
was . . . I was the one who pulled out . . . pulled
out the video recorder plug."

Edward started to howl. "I pulled out the plug
for the washing machine. I was only trying to
save energy like Maxine said we should."

"I never told you to pull out every plug in the
house," I protested. "Mum, that's not fair . . ."

"That's enough. Right then," Mum's hands
were on her hips. "All three of you are going

to clean up this kitchen until it's spotless. And all three of you will get no more pocket money until you've paid for my ruined jumpers."

And Mum marched out of the kitchen.

We got out the mop and some squeezy-cloths and started mopping up the floor.

"It's all your fault," Antony said.

"Yeah, *all* your fault," Edward agreed. "You were the one who came home and said we should save energy."

"It was your idea to check and make sure we'd saved energy before we went to bed," I told the twins.

"But it was your idea in the first place," Antony said.

"I'm not talking to you two," I said in a huff.

"And we're not talking to you either," Antony whinged. "Your idea was mega-super-duper-ginormous-galactic stinky. We didn't save our energy. My arms are killing me."

"Mine too," Edward agreed, giving me a dirty look.

Huh! Sometimes being a super heroine is no fun.

Beware the Park Bench

We were going to Aunt Joanne and Uncle Stan's house.

Their house is neat and clean and . . . really boring! They don't have one single book on the floor. They don't have any comics on the chairs. Their kitchen never has dirty forks and spoons lying about in the sink. It's not like our house at all.

We always have to dress up in our best clothes when we visit Uncle Stan and Aunt Joanne. Even Mum dresses up.

As it was a sunny day, Mum decided that we could walk through the park. Our aunt and uncle live just on the other side of the park. So off we went.

"Maxine, Antony, Edward, make sure you keep your clothes spotless," Mum warned. "So there is to be no messing about."

As if we would!

The park was full of people.

"Mum, can I go on the swings? Please, *please?*" I asked.

"No. You'll get your dress dirty," replied Mum.

"Mum, can I go on the roundabout?" Antony asked.

"Yeah! The roundabout," Edward repeated.

"No. You'll get your clothes creased," Mum said.

I didn't see the point of going through the park if you couldn't run and jump and play in the playground.

"Oh, look at that," I said.

Near us, a girl and a boy were flying a kite. It danced in the sky. We all stopped to watch.

"Mum, do you know how to make a kite?" I asked.

"Yes, I'll show you when we get back home. It's really easy," Mum said.

"Hooray!" we all shouted.

That cheered us up.

We were just passing by a park bench when I noticed something very strange. There were two spiders trying to swing down from the bench but they weren't getting very far. They scurried a little way along the bench and then tried to swing down but they never got all their legs off the bench. Then they scurried further along the bench and tried again but the same thing happened.

"How strange!" Mum said. "They can't get down."

And we all stopped to watch the spiders.

"Antony, Edward, do you know what I think?" I whispered to them.

"No, what?" Antony asked.

"Yeah! What?" Edward repeated.

So I said, "I think this is a job for Girl Wonder and . . ."

"The Terrific Twins!" my brothers whispered back.

And we spun around until the park was spinning with us.

"What on earth are you three doing?" Mum laughed.

"It's a secret," I told Mum.

"Well, come on. We can't stand here all day," Mum said.

"But Mum, can't we help the spiders?" Antony asked.

"Yeah! Can't we do something? They want to get down." Edward said.

"Oh, all right then," Mum replied.

She doesn't like spiders much. We all sat down on the bench and watched the spiders some more. Then I saw a piece of brown cardboard propped up against the side of the park bench.

"I've got a plan," I said to the twins as I leaned over to get it. "This piece of cardboard will help the spiders to get to the ground."

I leaned one end of the piece of cardboard against the bench and the other end I placed against the ground so that the piece of cardboard was like a slide.

"Come on, Mr and Mrs Spider," I said. "We haven't got all day."

"No, we haven't," Mum agreed, glancing down at her watch.

The spiders hopped on to the cardboard immediately and scuttled down to the ground.

"Come on, then," Mum said, and she went to stand up. Only she had trouble. It was like she was sticking to the bench.

"What on earth . . .?" Mum said.

She put her hand down on the bench. Then she looked at the palm of her hand. It was bright green.

"This bench is wet," Mum said, springing up off the bench. "Stand up you three."

We stood up.

"Turn around," Mum ordered.

We turned around.

"Oh no!" Mum cried. "Just look at your best clothes!"

We twisted our heads to look at our backs. I pulled the back of my dress skirt out to look at it. It was covered in green paint.

"Why didn't they leave a warning here to say the bench had just been painted?" Mum asked furiously, her hands on her hips.

She was seriously, *seriously* annoyed!

Then she looked down at the cardboard slide I had used to get the spiders to the ground. She picked it up and turned it over. Then showed it to us. There on the sign, in big green letters, it said: BEWARE!! WET PAINT!!

Maxine, where did you get this sign from?" Mum asked.

"From beside the bench," I replied.

"Why didn't you read it before we all sat down and ruined our clothes? That's why the spiders couldn't get down. Their feet kept sticking to the paint," Mum said. "Come on. We're going to have to go home and change before we can go anywhere."

"Look at my mega-terrific trousers," Antony said to me. "There's paint all over them."

"Yeah! Look at my super-mega-terrific trousers," Edward said. "I'll never be able to wear them again."

"You're plan was mega-useless," said Antony.

"Yeah! Super-duper-mega useless," said
Edward.

"But it worked, didn't it?" I said. "After all,
we *did* get the spiders off the bench."

About the author

Malorie Blackman has shot to fame since her first book was published in 1990. Many prizes have come her way, including the W. H. Smith Mind Boggling Award for *Hacker* and the Children's Book Award for her brilliant novel *Noughts and Crosses*, and she has been short-listed for the Carnegie Prize. Several of Malorie's books have been very successfully televised.

A former computer database manager, Malorie lives with her husband and daughter in South London and plays many different musical instruments in her spare time.

Other Barn Owl titles you might enjoy

ARABEL, MORTIMER AND THE ESCAPED BLACK MAMBA
by Joan Aiken and Quentin Blake

When Arabel and her irrepressible friend the raven Mortimer spend a fun-packed evening with their favourite baby-sitter, they have no idea of the chaos they will create in their wake.

While Arabel, Mortimer and Chris are out to buy a pint of milk, Arabel's parents return home and find the house empty and apparently ransacked. They fear the worst! Can it be the black mamba that has escaped from the zoo or has Arabel been kidnapped?

JIMMY JELLY
by Jacqueline Wilson

Young Angela is obsessed with Jimmy Jelly, her favourite T.V. personality. The rest of the family can't stand him. That is until Jimmy Jelly in person comes to open a shop in the local shopping mall!

A delightful tale from the master pen of Jacqueline Wilson.